£3.95

THOMAS
THE TANK ENGINE
& FRIENDS
ANNUAL

Based on the Railway Series by The Rev. W. Awdry

Written by Christopher Awdry
© William Heinemann Limited 1989

Cover illustration by Owain Bell
© Britt Allcroft (Thomas) Limited 1988

Endpaper illustration by Owain Bell
© Britt Allcroft (Thomas) Limited 1988

Other full colour illustrations by David Palmer
© Britt Allcroft (Thomas) Limited 1989

Line illustrations by Owain Bell
© Britt Allcroft (Thomas) Limited 1987

Photographic stills by David Mitton, Kenny McArthur and Terry Permane
from the television series "Thomas the Tank Engine & Friends"
© Britt Allcroft (Thomas) Limited 1984, 1986

All publishing rights: William Heinemann Limited. All television and merchandising rights
licensed by William Heinemann Limited to
Britt Allcroft (Thomas) Limited exclusively worldwide

Published by

GRANDREAMS,
Jadwin House,
205/211 Kentish Town Road,
London NW5 2JU.

Printed in Italy

ISBN 0 86227 674 8

CONTENTS

Hello!

A few weeks ago, I went to visit Sodor. The Fat Controller agreed with my request, but as I approached the engine shed I heard raised voices from inside. The voices sounded as if they were arguing.

"....it's disgusting," said a voice which could only have been Gordon's. "There have been five Annuals now, and they've all been introduced by one of the Branch Line engines - Thomas, Toby or somebody. Branch lines are all very well in their way," the voice went on, "and I'm not saying that you get a junior engine, but ..."

At that point I opened the door. The voices died away.

"Good morning," I said. "I presume, in that case, that you wouldn't wish to mix with such engines in introducing the next Annual, would you?"

The silence grew longer.

"Er ..." began Henry at last.

"But ..." said James.

"Well, you see ..." rumbled Gordon.

I waited, hoping for more, but they said nothing.

"The Fat Controller," I announced, "has sent me to ask if Gordon would like to do the

Introduction for this year's Annual, but since he seems to have such strong views about the other ones, perhaps ..."

"No, no, not at all," interrupted Gordon hurriedly. "I'd be delighted." Henry and James exchanged winks, and I tried hard not to smile.

"What's it about this year?" Gordon added.

"There's quite a lot about trucks," I said.

"Trucks!" exclaimed Gordon indignantly. "I mean, trucks," he went on more quietly, no doubt afraid that I might change my mind and ask somebody else. "Er ... got the stories there, have you?"

I handed them over. There was silence for a while.

After a little, Gordon chuckled.

"Old Square Wheels," he murmured with a reminiscent smile.

"What's that?" asked Henry suspiciously.

"Oh, nothing," said Gordon, and went on reading.

Leaving the stories, I crept quietly away. Gordon seemed to be enjoying them - turn the page, and I'm sure you will to. There's also pictures of all your favourite engines and plenty of puzzles too!

Thomas, Percy and Toby listened anxiously as the summer gale rattled the windows and moaned in the roof of the engine shed. Gradually the moan rose to a howl. There was a crack and a slithering noise on the roof as a slate broke and slid into the guttering. The engines shivered.

When their crews came to start work the next morning the engines had had very little sleep.

"There's a mountain railway I've heard of," said Thomas hopefully, "where the trains stop running if it's windy because it's too dangerous."

His driver laughed.

"Sorry Thomas," he said. "To begin with, you weigh much more than those little engines, and secondly wind is usually far worse up in the mountains."

Thomas soon found that the wind was not only strong, but cold too. Annie and Clarabel didn't like it any more than he did, but grumbled not because of the wind, but because there weren't many passengers. Thomas didn't blame the

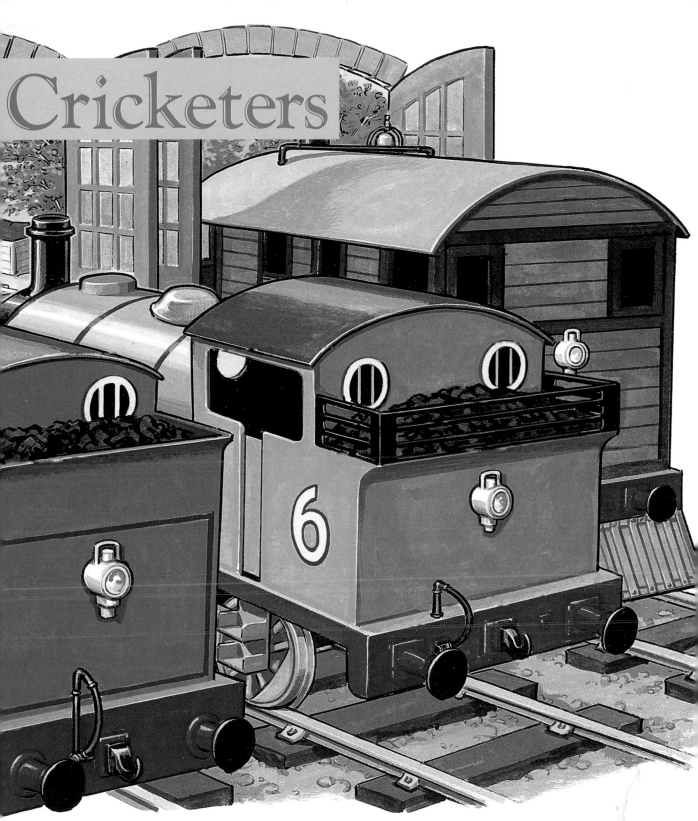

Cricketers

passengers for staying at home. He wished he could have done the same.

Yet as they passed the cricket field near the station by the river, Thomas was amazed to see white-clad figures playing.

"It's an important match," explained his fireman, who played cricket himself when he had the time. "The final of the Sodor Knockout Competition. But I don't envy them in this wind."

Trees between the railway and

cricket field swayed wildly in the wind as Thomas ran past. One of the players recognised the fireman, and waved. The fireman waved back, but he was glad to be in the shelter of Thomas's cab today.

At the Junction, James told them about the trouble that the wind had caused all over the island.

"Let's get home as quickly as we can," said Thomas when James had gone. They reached the middle station safely and stopped. Only two passengers got out, and Thomas whistled and set off again. By the time he reached the curve which led round the cricket field they were going nicely.

"Come along now, come along now," he puffed confidently to Annie and Clarabel. "Not far now," he said to himself. "We'll soon be back in our warm shed."

He was halfway round the bend when a flash of white caught his eye. Almost at once the train brakes went on, as the Guard pulled the emergency cord. With a squeal Thomas slowed and stopped, but not before he had rounded the curve far enough to see a huge tree lying across the line.

"Phew!" he exclaimed. "How did the Guard know about that?"

His driver looked back, and saw some cricketers running towards them, followed by the Guard.

"Thank goodness!" panted the cricketers. "We heard Thomas whistle as he left the station, and just then we saw the tree come down. We didn't think we'd be in time. I'm glad we were."

"So are we," remarked the fireman. "Thank you."

And since Thomas could go no further until the tree was cleared, his driver and fireman took him back to the middle station. Then, while Bertie took the passengers home, they watched the rest of the cricket match, which the local team won after a close and exciting finish.

A few days later, at a meeting in the cricket pavilion, the Fat Controller presented the cricketers with a framed certificate to remind them of the day they saved the train.

The cricketers are almost prouder of this, than their cricket trophy. "Next year," said the captain of the team, "we may have to pass the cricket cup to someone else. But your certificate will always be here."

Edward

James

A PICTURE TO PAINT

Hosepipes And Shunters

Mavis, the Quarry Company's diesel engine had gone away for repairs, and Toby was doing her work in the quarry. One morning Percy was shunting in the Yard at Ffarquhar when the Stationmaster came to see him.

"There's an emergency at the Harbour," he said. "The Fat Controller wants you to go at once, to help sort it out."

"But what about this shunting?" Percy protested. "Toby is up at the quarry, and the shunting must be done."

"Never mind that," said the Stationmaster. "Off you go, we'll manage the shunting somehow. And," he added to himself as he hurried back to his office, "thanks to Toby's stories about the old days I know how."

Terence's owner was enjoying his morning coffee break in the farmhouse kitchen when the telephone rang.

"Bother!" he said. "Why do they always have to choose now?"

His wife answered the ringing, and listened.

"It's the Stationmaster," she said, handing the receiver to the farmer. When he heard what the Stationmaster had to say, he nodded.

"Why not?" he said. "We've nothing here that can't wait a day or two. We'll be with you in about half an hour, though I don't see how you're going to work it."

When Terence and his owner reached the station yard they found the Stationmaster waiting. Beside him, on the ground, lay a framework made of wood.

Terence's owner jumped down.

"How ...?" he began.

"We fix this frame to Terence's front," explained the Stationmaster, "so that he can push. When he needs to pull, we use a cable from his towbar. The shunters will tell you where the trucks need to go. Oh, and if you need to cross any of the lines, please use those metal ramps."

Terence had the time of his life. The trucks grumbled, but then trucks always do. Terence took no notice of them.

"If Toby could see me now," he chuckled to himself.

But up at the quarry, Toby had other things on his mind. He had worked hard all morning, and as he had only a small water-tank, it was now nearly empty. Unfortunately, because Mavis did not need much water, the water-column that had once stood near the office had been taken away.

"Bother that Mavis," grumbled Toby. "Why can't she drink water like any proper engine, instead of that horrible oily stuff? What am I going to do now?"

Toby's driver laughed.

"It's not her fault, is it," he pointed out. "She can't help the way she was constructed."

Toby was unconvinced.

"There must be water somewhere," he said desperately. He knew that without it his fire would have to be put out and he would be stranded at the quarry until he was rescued. He didn't fancy the idea of Mavis's lonely shed.

"There's a tap in the quarryman's restroom," the Quarrymaster told them doubtfully, "and another here in the kitchen. You're welcome to them."

"Splendid," said the fireman, rubbing his hands. "Now all we need is a hosepipe."

"There's one in my shed at home," said a shunter, and went off to fetch it. He returned with a rusty reel, with some very old-looking hosepipe wound on it.

"It'll have to do," said the fireman as he uncoiled it. He fastened one end to the tap and put the other into Toby's tank. Then he turned to the driver, who was standing by the tap. "I'd like 625 gallons, please,"

he said.

"Very good, Sir," said the driver, and switched the water on.

Toby's tank was small, but it took a very long time to fill. By the time they had finished, he was late with his work, and it was dark before he got back to Ffarquhar.

"Quarries are all very well," he grumbled as he fell asleep, "but you'd think a poor engine would be able to get a quick drink. Is it so much to ask?"

The Fat Controller

Harold

The Railway QUIZ

ANSWERS ON PAGES 60-61

4. How many wheels has Henry (above) got?

1. Above: Which engine is number 10?

2. Who once pulled a truck in half?

3. What colour is Duck?

5. What is Toby's coach called?

6. Who, above, was once fooled by a 'backing signal'?

9. Who took Thomas's passengers home when Thomas got stuck in a snowdrift?

7. Whom did Edward, above, rescue from a scrapyard?

8. What number is Gordon?

10. Which engine couldn't pull his train without a leather bootlace?

The Fat Controller had borrowed a diesel. He told Duck to show the new engine round, but Diesel made mistakes, and the trucks began singing cheeky songs about him.

Trucks are waiting in the Yard; tackling them with ease'll,

"Show the world what I can do," gaily boasts the Diesel.

In and out he creeps about, like a big black weasel,

When he pulls the wrong trucks out, Pop goes the Diesel!

Duck was cross, and told the trucks to stop, but Diesel thought the song was Duck's fault.

"I'll pay him out," Diesel said to himself, but he couldn't think how.

"It's not fair," he complained to Henry, Gordon and James. "I never get a moment's peace from these rude trucks, and it's all because of that Duck!"

"Nonsense," said Henry. "Duck would never do that. It would be des...des..."

"Disgraceful!" put in Gordon.

"Disgusting!" said James.

"Despicable!" finished Henry.

Diesel was not convinced. He spent the rest of the day wondering how he would get his own back.

Next day, Henry's trucks chattered amongst themselves, and paid no attention to him. They were very full and wanted to take it out on someone. "Why not Henry?" they whispered to each other.

"Wait until I give the word," said the front truck.

At last the signal went down.

"Come on you," Henry ordered shortly. Reluctantly, and still chattering, the trucks followed him

Old Square

out of the Yard.

All went well until they reached the top of the hill.

"Steady," Henry warned the trucks. They heard, but they took no notice.

"Now!" shouted the front truck.

"Go on, go on!" yelled the trucks as, surging against Henry's tender,

Wheels

they pushed as hard as they could.

"Stop, stop!" wailed Henry, and his driver braked as hard as he dared. But Henry couldn't hold the heavy trucks properly - his wheels locked, and he slithered, out of control, down the hill with the stupid trucks cheering and shouting behind him.

"Help, help!" whistled Henry despairingly.

Thomas, waiting in the branch line platform, saw Henry coming, but could do nothing to help. But the hill ended before reaching the station, and Henry was at last able to bring the silly trucks under control. Gradually his driver eased off the brakes. When he was sure that the trucks were behaving themselves, Henry came to a controlled stop.

"Phew!" he said. "What stupid things trucks are - they could have caused an accident."

"Never mind," said Thomas. "They didn't, that's the main thing. You did well to stop them."

Thomas puffed away, and after a while Henry set off again. But something strange seemed to have happened to his wheels. Each time they went round there was a 'clunk' when they reached a certain spot.

"What's that?" he asked after a while.

"You've got a flat tyre," said the driver.

"What?" objected Henry indignantly. "Engines don't get flat tyres. Only cars and lorries - and buses like Bertie - get them."

His driver laughed.

"It's the trucks' fault," he explained. "All that sliding on the hill, with your wheels locked in the same place, has worn a flat place on each of your driving wheels. You'll have to go to the Works, I'm afraid."

They clunked to the end of the line, and Henry went crossly to the Shed. Duck was there, and Diesel.

"What's the matter, Henry?" asked Duck. "Those trucks been playing you up, have they?"

"Yes, they have," snorted Henry.

"Pushed me down the hill, and now Driver says I've got flat tyres."

"Ah," said Duck. "Bumpy, that. But you can't trust trucks, can you. Ah well, I hope you get your 'flats' sorted out all right." And he puffed off to see about the next train.

Diesel sniggered. He'd just had an idea. Next day he spoke to the trucks.

"That was a good trick you played on Henry," he said. "He's got flat tyres now, and has gone to the Works to have them replaced." He paused. "I shouldn't really tell you this," he went on quietly, "but I know you won't pass it on. Do you know Duck's new nickname for Henry? Old Square Wheels. Good isn't it? Don't tell anyone I told you."

The trucks promised, but as Duck had said, you cannot trust trucks. When Henry came back from the Works the whisper went round.

"Here's Old Square Wheels," it said. "Old Square Wheels is back."

As Diesel had expected, it was only a matter of time before the trucks told Henry that Duck had invented the nickname.

"I'll give him Duck," Henry said furiously. "Just wait till I see him again!"

The trucks sniggered, and Diesel smirked with satisfaction.

"That worked well," he said to himself. "Now, what can I think up about Gordon?"

There are 10 differences in these two pictures. Can you spot them?
Answers on pages 60-61.

Trevor

Daisy

WORD SEARCH

The following 22 characters associated with Thomas The Tank Engine are all hidden in the grid below. Using a pen or pencil, how many can you find? They may be hidden forwards, backwards, up, down or diagonally - but always in a straight line. Answers on pages 60 - 61.

THOMAS
DONALD
HAROLD
BILL
DUCK
CLARABEL

TREVOR
DOUGLAS
DIESEL
BEN
ANNIE
TERENCE

FAT CONTROLLER
DAISY
PERCY
JAMES
BOCO

TOBY
EDWARD
GORDON
BERTIE
TRUCK

F	A	T	C	O	N	T	R	O	L	L	E	R	R	D
F	E	O	P	Q	T	O	X	W	A	B	I	D	J	O
X	C	V	O	C	O	B	K	L	E	D	N	P	S	N
A	N	D	A	I	S	Y	Y	E	D	I	N	L	N	A
T	E	L	Q	W	E	O	D	S	W	P	A	A	F	L
X	R	O	T	A	C	E	L	S	A	L	G	U	O	D
H	E	R	N	Y	L	R	J	I	R	W	O	J	Y	P
K	T	A	F	C	A	M	A	J	D	F	U	G	T	O
N	I	H	M	R	R	Q	M	I	W	V	G	X	Z	A
S	Y	T	E	E	A	H	E	J	E	N	O	R	S	K
A	G	M	Q	P	B	S	S	P	B	E	R	T	I	E
M	U	D	P	B	E	F	C	U	Q	R	D	N	T	L
O	V	O	D	L	L	I	B	W	T	D	O	U	O	J
H	Z	A	C	X	E	Y	E	X	C	P	N	D	C	M
T	R	E	V	O	R	Z	N	R	A	T	R	U	C	K

Thomas

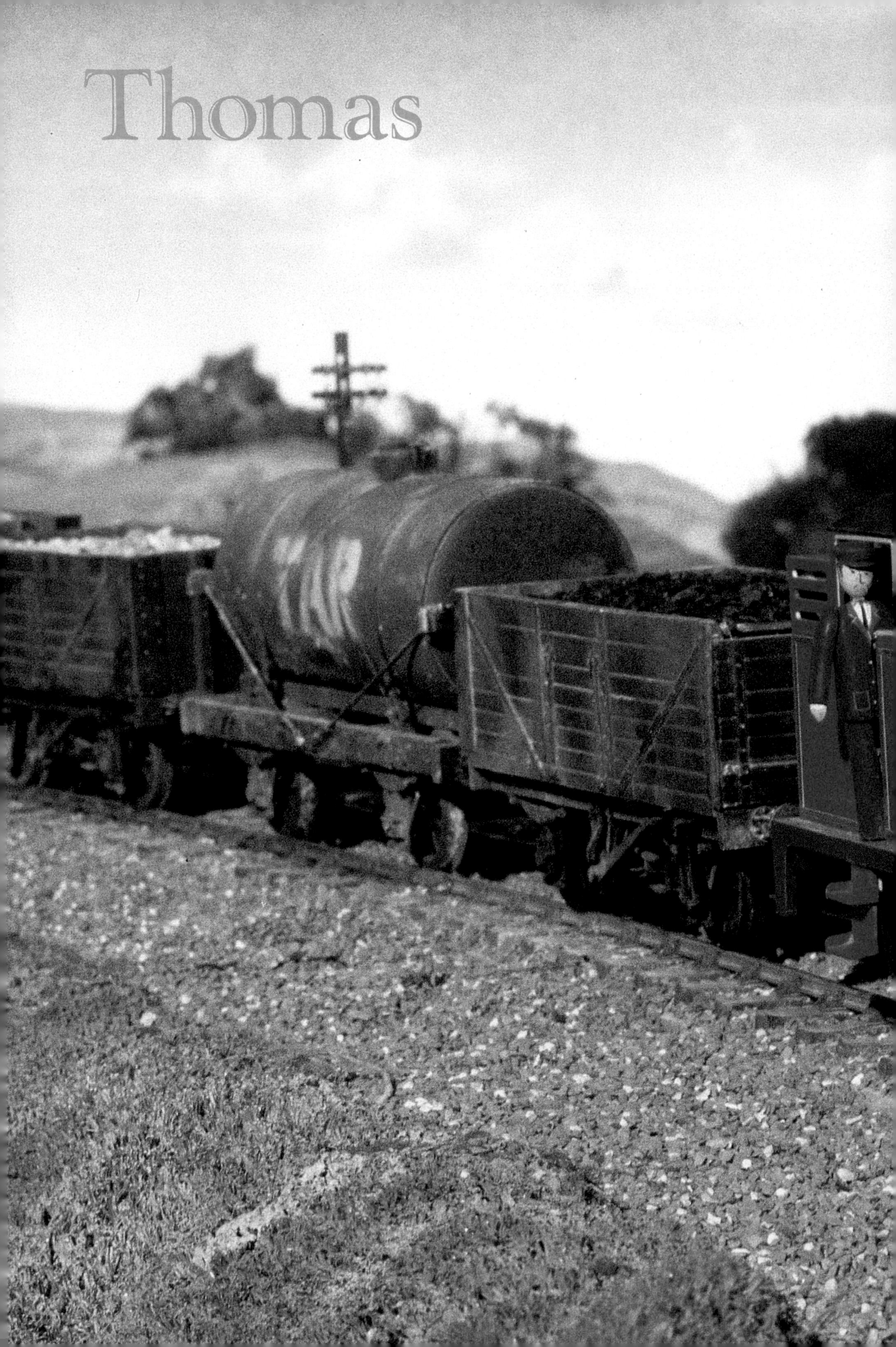

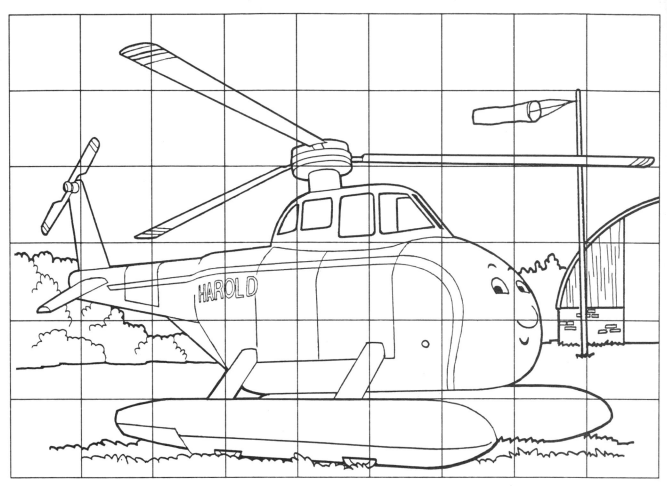

Draw in the picture of Harold in the space below, using the squares as a guide. Then colour both pictures in.

The Fat Controller's Ticket Twister

The printers have mixed up all the placenames on the Fat Controller's new batch of tickets. Can you help to sort them out?

A. MUDHITTO-SANGERVOCAT
B. GRANSTOVECA-ROLEASKY
C. DROPFANK-RHARQUAFF
D. CIVARSNOWT-NOKKARIRN
E. SLADEREAL-GRUBSHALER
F. SLOWTHREWL-MERBAND

1. ARLESDALE-ARLESBURGH
2. KNAPFORD-FFARQUHAR
3. VICARSTOWN-KIRK RONAN
4. WELLSWORTH-BRENDAM
5. TIDMOUTH-CROVANS GATE
6. CROVANS GATE-SKARLOEY

Answers on pages 60-61.

Toby

Bill and Ben

Donald And The Breakaways

Donald and Douglas, the Scottish twins did not mind what job they did. Coaches or trucks, it was all the same to them. Which meant, as often as not, that they pulled trucks, since the big engines all disliked them.

"You don't really like them, do you?" James asked in amazement one day.

"Och, it's all wurrk," remarked Douglas. "If we didna dae it, some ither body wud."

James marvelled. He hated trucks himself, but he had to admit that Donald and Douglas managed to make them behave better than anyone else did. The secret, of course, was that the trucks had not forgotten an incident when Donald had smashed a rude brake-van. It had been an accident really, but no-one told the trucks and they still thought that Donald had done it on purpose.

"Keep on the right side of those

38

two," the trucks had said to each other when either of the Twins was about.

One day, Donald had to take empty trucks to the Other Railway and bring back loaded ones. The 'empties' behaved well, and when Donald reached the Big Station he was feeling good.

"We've got those trucks licked into shape," he congratulated himself. What he didn't realise was that the loaded ones he was about to take

back were visitors, and had never been 'licked into shape' by anybody.

"What's this?" they screeched when Donald backed on to them. "We want a proper engine, not an old-fashioned steam-kettle."

They should, of course, have known better, but then trucks never do.

"Old-fashioned!" snorted Donald. "I'll teach you a lesson. Take that." He gave the trucks a hard bump.

The trucks sniggered.

"He's cross," they whispered. "Let's have some fun."

They behaved well for a while, and Donald began to think he had them under control. Like the trucks, he should have known better. By the time they reached the Works station, an axle-box on one of the trucks had 'run hot', and they had to shunt that one off the train. At the next station the guard had to fasten a brake-rod which had slipped on, 'accidentally on purpose'. One delay followed another, and Donald became crosser and crosser.

"Stupid things!" he scolded. But the trucks didn't care.

"What does he know about it?" they asked each other. "We're modern, we are not out-of-date like his sort. Steam-kettle! Huh!"

At the top of Gordon's Hill, Donald stopped so that the brakes could be checked along the train.

Unfortunately he restarted more

40

WORD SEARCH

```
F A T C O N T R O L L E R R D
F E O P Q T O X W A B I D J O
X C V O C O B K L E D N P S N
A N D A I S Y Y E D I N L N A
T E L Q W E O D S W P A A F L
X R O T A C E L S A L G U O D
H E R N Y L R J I R W O J Y P
K T A F C A M A J D F U G T O
N I H M R R Q M I W V G X Z A
S Y T E E A H E J E N O R S K
A G M Q P B S S P B E R T I E
M U D P B E F C U Q R D N T L
O V O D L L I B W T D O U O J
H Z A C X E Y E X C P N D C M
T R E V O R Z N R A T R U C K
```

The Railway QUIZ

The Fat Controller's Ticket Twister

ANSWERS

SPOT THE DIFFERENCE

Gordon

Henry

A PICTURE TO PAINT

A PICTURE TO PAINT

them to let James out he found he couldn't. He was most apologetic.

"The lock must have jammed," he said. "I'm afraid James will have to stay where he is - no, hang on, he can't. Edward needs to use that platform in a quarter of an hour. We'll have to put James out of the way in the goods yard."

James was not pleased, and neither were his passengers. Bertie came to take them to their proper stations, but James stood in the siding with nothing to do for the rest of the day.

That evening the Fat Controller came to see him.

"I'm sorry, James," he said, "but mending those points is going to take longer than I thought. Meanwhile, Edward needs help, and since you can't...er...escape, you may as well do something useful."

"Yes, sir," agreed James.

At first James quite enjoyed it. But as time went on, knowing exactly what he had to do, and when, became rather dull. In fact, he was delighted when the points were at last mended and the Fat Controller said he could go back to the Big Shed.

It was late when he reached it. Gordon opened a sleepy eye.

"Hullo," he said. "You've sorted Edward's branch line out for him then? That's good."

James didn't answer. He didn't go so far as Gordon in thinking that branch lines were vulgar, but he did agree with him on the subject of freedom.

"Just you wait," he muttered. "I'll show you."

James came cautiously down Gordon's Hill because he knew he had to stop at Edward's station which lay near the bottom. It was lucky he did, because just before they reached the platform James noticed that the points were directing them into the branch platform instead of the main one.

"Stop!" he whistled, and his driver quickly put on the brakes.

James was not going fast, but suddenly he realised that the platform ended with buffers.

"Help!" he gasped, and shut his eyes. When the crash didn't come he opened them again and found that he had stopped with a few inches to spare.

"All right, James," said the fireman. "I'll ask the signalman to put us back on the proper line. I won't be long."

The signalman had reset the points behind James, as the rules said, but when he tried to change

53

say that because you were once turned on to Edward's branch by mistake."

Gordon closed his eyes. His branch line incident was not one he wished to remember.

Soon James's driver and fireman came for him. James bustled away importantly, and Henry and Gordon exchanged knowing grins.

When he passed Edward's station, James told Edward how much he would like a branch line.

"You can come and help me any

time," smiled Edward. "With BoCo away I've been worked off my wheels just lately."

James sighed as he set off again. The rest of his journey was uneventful. James kept good time, and was feeling quite pleased with himself as he set off for home once more.

At the Works station he met Gordon.

"Found any good branch lines?" Gordon chuckled.

James took no notice.

No Return

One morning, James's driver came early to the Shed.

"There's a change of plan, James," he said. "We're to take the stopping passenger train today, not the goods train, so we must be ready half an hour earlier."

James was glad to be taking coaches rather than trucks, but he was not so pleased about the extra hurry. Henry and Gordon were in the Shed too.

"It would be nice to have a branch line to myself," remarked James wistfully.

"You!" exclaimed the others in one voice.

"Why not?" demanded James. "At least I'd know where my next load was coming from."

"Ah," said Gordon knowingly, "but what about all the trucks?" Gordon hated trucks, and had once run off a turntable to avoid pulling them.

"And there's the shunting," put in Henry. "You'd have to do your own, you know."

"Well..." James hesitated. He had to admit that shunting was what he liked least. "Perhaps Donald or Douglas would do it for me..." he began, "...or perhaps not," he finished lamely seeing the pitying looks of the others. "Anyway, branch lines aren't so bad. I can't think why you don't like them, Gordon."

"I like my freedom," said Gordon. "I need a good run for my wheels, scope to use my talents. You wouldn't understand, little James," he said grandly.

"Pooh!" scoffed James. "You only

Percy

Draw in the picture of Trevor in the space below, using the squares as a guide. Then colour both pictures in.

Duck

Diesel

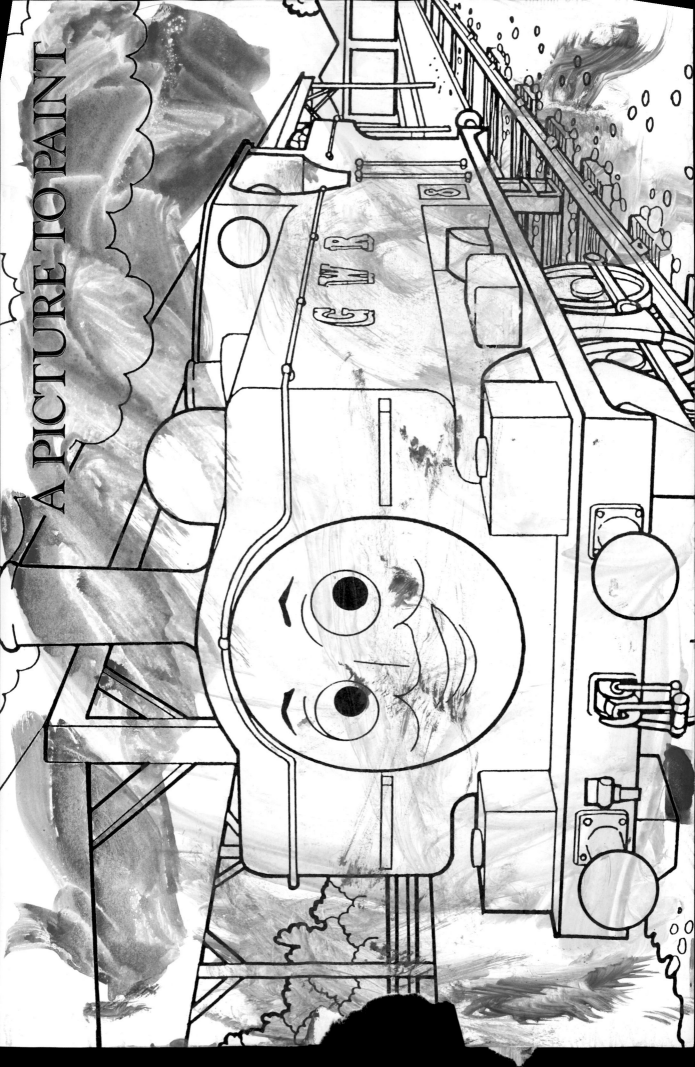

A PICTURE TO PAINT

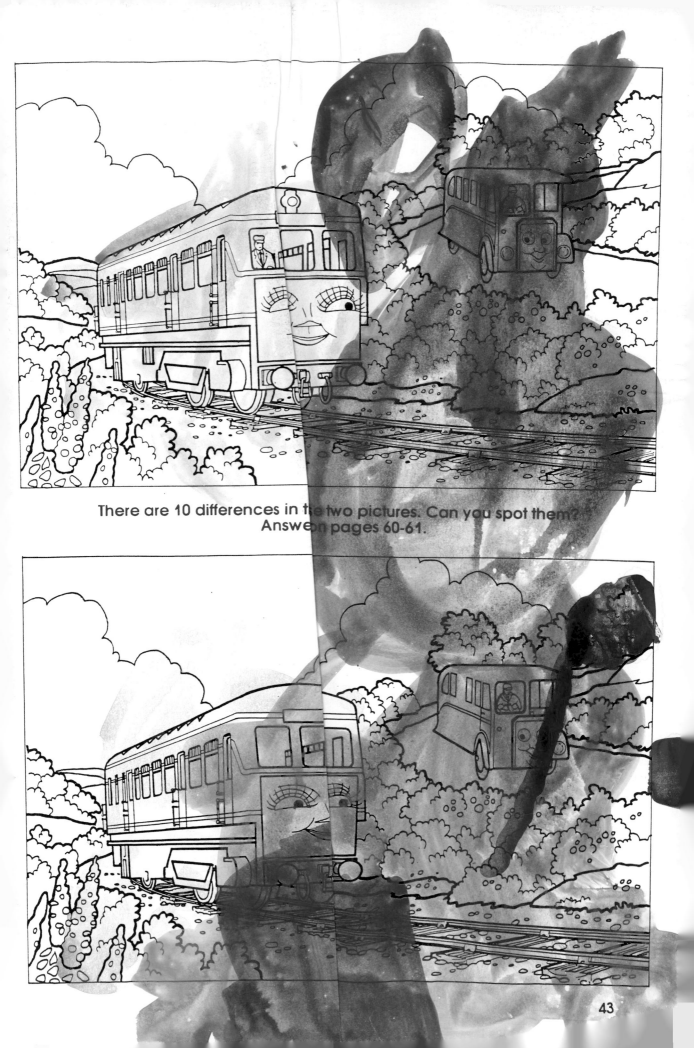

There are 10 differences in the two pictures. Can you spot them? Answer on pages 60-61.

43

Quickly the signalman summed up the situation. He set the line ahead as far as he could, and Donald clattered safely by. Then came the trucks, but the signalman saw with relief that they were slowing down by the time they reached him. With a groan of relief they stopped, just beyond the station platform. The signalman sent out an 'Obstruction, danger' warning and set all his signals to 'stop'.

Then he waited.

When he was sure that the trucks had stopped, Donald stopped too, half a mile further on.

"We shall need permission to go back," the driver told the fireman. "Nip back and clear it with the signalman, please."

When he had permission, Donald was able to go carefully back towards the trucks. He bumped them fiercely.

"Now will you behave?" he growled.

This time the trucks had scared even themselves.

"Yes, we will," they quavered uncertainly.

And Donald finished his journey with no more trouble at all.

quickly than he meant to, and the jerk broke an old coupling-hook ten trucks from the end.

Feeling the snatch, Donald's fireman looked back. They were already a little way down the hill, but, coming after them, and gathering speed on the slope, he saw the last ten trucks.

"We've got to keep ahead of them, Donald," he said. "Quick now - I just hope there's nothing in the platform at Edward's station."

"But we're supposed to stop there and leave some of these trucks," objected Donald.

"Can't help that," replied his driver. "If those trucks catch us we'll stop even earlier because they'll knock us off the rails."

"What are we waiting for then?" asked Donald, and put on speed.

It was touch and go for a while. If the guard's brake had not been holding the breakaways slightly, Donald could not have kept ahead. But he managed it - just! They saw Edward's station in front. Whistling loudly, Donald raced towards it, while the trucks followed, screaming with fright.

41